When Someone is Afraid

By
Valeri Gorbachev

Illustrated by
Kostya Gorbachev

STAR BRIGHT BOOKS
CAMBRIDGE MASSACHUSETTS

Published by Star Bright Books.

The name Star Bright Books and the Star Bright Books logo are registered trademarks
of Star Bright Books, Inc. Please visit www.starbrightbooks.com.
For bulk orders, please email: orders@starbrightbooks.com, or call (617) 354-1300.

English Hardback ISBN 13: 978-1-932065-99-2
English Hardback ISBN 10: 1-932065-99-7
Star Bright Books/MA/00103160
Printed in China (WKT) 9 8 7 6 5 4 3

English Paperback ISBN: 978-1-59572-344-4
Star Bright Books/MA/00103160
Printed in China (WKT) 9 8 7 6 5 4 3 2

Printed on paper from sustainable forests.

Library of Congress Cataloging-in-Publication Data

Gorbachev, Valeri.
 When someone is afraid / by Valeri & Kostya Gorbachev.
  p. cm.
Summary: Suggests some of the ways that animals react to fear, but when a small boy wakes
from a bad dream he calls for his mommy and daddy.
ISBN 1-932065-99-7
[1. Fear--Fiction. 2. Fear of the dark--Fiction. 3. Dreams--Fiction.] I. Gorbachev, Kostya, ill. II. Title.
PZ7.G6475Wg 2004
[E]--dc22

2004017158

When an ostrich is afraid. . .

it buries its head in the sand.

When a giraffe is afraid. . .

it runs away as fast as it can.

When fish are afraid. . .

they dart away.

When frogs are afraid. . .

they dive into a pond.

When crows are afraid. . .

they fly away.

When a rabbit is afraid. . .

it races into the bushes.

When a turtle is afraid. . .

it shrinks into its shell.

When a squirrel is afraid. . .

it scampers up a tree.

When a mouse is afraid. . .

it hurries into a hole.

When my kitten is afraid. . .

she hides under my bed.

When my dog is afraid. . .

he hides behind me.

When I get scared,
I call Mommy or Daddy.

"What's wrong,
honey?"

"I had a
bad dream."

Mommy gives me a hug. . .

and a kiss. . .

and I am not afraid anymore.